Sweet Dreams, I Love You

D0490783

bookoli

"It's getting late,
it's time for bed,
To snuggle up
and rest your head."

Little Otter wants to stay,

he doesn't feel sleepy.

"Can't we play

inside my teepee?"

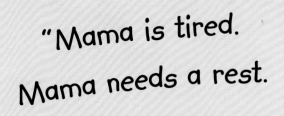

"Mama is tired.
Mama needs a rest.

"Does your teepee have room for an overnight guest?"

"Yes, of course!
I'll make you a bed,
With a big, comfy quilt
and a pillow for your head."

Mama sees something
hanging overhead,
With feathers and beads
and a web of black thread.

"My dream catcher

grabs the bad dreams

in the night.

Then they all fly away

when it starts to get light.

"And here are the feathers,

which hang over my bed.

They help the good dreams

float into my head."

Little Otter touches the feathers,

a dream starts to swirl.

It's Otter the Astronaut
zooming out of this world!

"Some nights I'm at the circus, flying on a trapeze,

Doing flips in the air, swinging through the breeze.

"Or I'm diving underwater with dolphins and whales,

Getting octopus hugs as I wave to the snails."

"Another dream
is when I'm quite small,

PLAYING CARDS

"And my best friend's a mouse who lives in the wall."

"Another dream I love,"
Otter says, lying back.
"Is floating in a pool
with a drink and a snack."

Then Little Otter gets quiet.
He doesn't make a peep.
As he talks about dreams,
he drifts off to sleep!

"Time to sleep now,
I hope your dreams all come true.

Good night, little one.
Sweet dreams, I love you."